Enrico Valle, Frederic P. Garesché

A Family of Martyrs

A Drama

Enrico Valle, Frederic P. Garesché

A Family of Martyrs
A Drama

ISBN/EAN: 9783337376864

Printed in Europe, USA, Canada, Australia, Japan

Cover: Foto ©Andreas Hilbeck / pixelio.de

More available books at **www.hansebooks.com**

A FAMILY OF MARTYRS.

A Drama,

BY

REV. ENRICO VALLE,

OF THE SOCIETY OF JESUS.

Translated from the Italian,

BY

REV. F. P. GARESCHE,

OF THE SAME SOCIETY.

CINCINNATI:

PUBLISHED BY J. P. WALSH,

170 SYCAMORE STREET.

1864.

PREFACE.

———◆———

THIS drama is not founded on fact. Although many similar incidents are to be found in the Acts of the Martyrs, I thought it better not to select any particular one, but to express, as well as I could, the heroic character of the primitive Christian, in his language, his firmness and his triumph. My only scope was to give pleasure to youth, by furnishing them, in the time of the Carnival, an innocent and useful amusement; this alone induced me to undertake this little work. Some of the students who belong to the Sodality of St. Aloysius, in the Roman College, took upon themselves the task of representing it, with the design of contributing to the recreation of their comrades; it was a part of my plan.

The favor with which it was received by the audience, and the authority of some, in whose judgment and sincerity I place the greatest confidence,

have prevailed upon me to give it to the printer,
contrary to my own inclinations, which would restrain me from publishing, partly from a feeling of
diffidence in myself, and partly from a sense of that
respect which is due to the public.

With the exception of a few trifling changes, it is
offered here such as it was at its representation.
And, although I fear that its success, on that occa-
sion, was owing to the ingenuous and touching man-
ner of the youthful actors, rather than to its own
intrinsic merits, I allow myself to entertain the hope
that my motives in writing it may avail to soften the
criticism of the reader, and that it may contribute
to further my original design—the amusement of the
young, for whose pleasure and instruction it was
composed.

ENRICO VALLE, S. J.

Rome, 1863.

DRAMATIS PERSONÆ.

——◆——

SEVERUS, ...	*A Roman citizen.*
SYLVANUS, ...	*His son.*
FAUSTINUS, . . .	*A younger son.*
VALENTIUS, ...	*Prefect of Rome.*
PUBLIUS, ...	*His son.*
ASTERIUS, ...	*A freedman of Severus.*
DEMETRIUS, . . .	*A pagan pontiff.*

Guards, lictors.

The action is at Rome: the change of scene being indicated at the proper places.

ACT I.

SCENE I.—*Catacombs.*

Sylvanus, Faustinus.

Sylv. Behold, Faustinus, these the catacombs,
Where silence holds her undisputed sway.

Faust. Sylvanus, I'm afraid. These hidden caves,
These tortuous paths; this atmosphere, that seems
The breath of death; the silence and the gloom—
Thrill me with terrors never felt before.

Sylv. No place is this for fear! 'T is sacred silence, and
The gloom is hallowed shade. Faustinus, here
The altars stand, on which celestial manna falls—
No earthly food—no figure, as of yore—
Christ's precious flesh and blood—the food of souls.

And here, when tyrants open wide the door
Of life, the fleshly garment of the soul,
All useless then, is laid in honored rest.

FAUST. And did they bring my mother's body here?

SYLV. They did: our mother sealed her faith with blood,
And left us martyrdom for legacy—
O happy memory, to hold such days!
Too young wert thou to see, through forked flames,
That mother's face, which wore the smile of heaven.
                              [FAUSTINUS *weeps.*]
What, brother! weeping?—whilst in Paradise
Her soul resplendent glories in the death
That was her triumph?

FAUST.   Ah! at least could I
But clasp my mother's form; upon the urn
That holds her sacred spoils imprint the kiss,
Which, in my dreams, I press upon her brow!

SYLV. The wish is holy, but, alas! in vain.
With those who then stood on the sacred pyre,
Companions still, her mingled ashes rest.
None know the place.

FAUST.   Not e'en Asterius?

SYLV. He sought in vain. The pious soul, who gave
Them honored sepulture, next sought these shades,
By others borne; himself a mangled form.
But this I know; to me the air is sweet,
As though I felt my mother's breath; and here,
Each softened echo seems her whispered tone.
    And thee, a Christian and a son, I bring
To venerate this spot, twice consecrate;
To seek new strength for danger that impends.

FAUST. What danger?

SYLV.   From Numidia returns
Our father to his native home. Our time
Of combat, long foreseen, at last has come.
That father, wandering in the shades of death,
Is all unconscious that his loved sons,
Through the baptismal waters' sacred fount,
Have left his errors for the sake of Christ.
What pangs, what agony, shall rack his heart;
What wiles, and snares, and struggles then,
To wrench us from our constancy and faith.

FAUST. What then ? Sylvanus, dost thou fear for me ?
No ! Heaven's smile shall hide my father's frown.

SYLV. The soft entreaties of a father's love,
More than a father's anger, move the hearts
Of loving sons—those blandishments I fear.

FAUST. No need. My mother shields me, and her death
Outweighs with me a living father's love.

SYLV. But who comes here ?

FAUST. (*Starting to run.*) Where can we flee !

SYLV.   Nay, stop—
It seems—it is—the prefect's son. Fear not ;
Myself did trust him with the secret clue.

[*Enter* PUBLIUS.]

SCENE II.

SYLVANUS, FAUSTINUS, PUBLIUS.

PUB. Once more well met ! In vain the forum, baths,
And gardens I explore ; these caves alone
Attract thy feet. What secret charm is here ?

Sylv. A charm indeed, for here our treasures lie.
Here peace is found, and life, and here alone,
Where all is dark and still, the Christian soul
May shun the sights and sounds of lustful Rome

Pub. I envy, though I can not follow thee.
Of faith diverse, my heart with pity melts,
Whene'er I think your sorrows o'er.   I hate
Maxentius, who sprinkles with your blood
The forum's marble and the dusty road.
And were not duty there, and filial love,
Ye gods forgive! I could my very father hate.

Sylv. Oh, speak not thus!

Pub.   Enforcing cruel laws,
The pliant tool of tyranny, he shares——

Sylv. No more!   He is thy father, and a son
Is cursèd, who but breathes his father's shame.

Pub. (*Embarrassed.*) Yes, thou art right. 'T is friend-
           ship that deceives.
She paints my father with a darker shade,

Reserving all her brighter tints for thee.
The gods themselves must share with thee my heart.

SYLV. In vain thy words assure to me a love,
Which is not, can not be my own.

PUB.   My friend,
Such words from thee ! so little merited !

SYLV. And where, O Publius, is thy proof of love ?
Not words, but deeds, alone, affection prove.
How long dost turn an adder's ear to me ?
How oft I vainly sought to lead thee from
The darkness that enshrines thy pagan gods,
To where the truth, like summer's blazing sun,
Assails thy willing blindness with its rays !
How oft with solemn oath thou hast assured——

PUB. 'T is true.   And yet I merit not reproach,
Am I thy enemy ?   Do I ensnare
The Christian, or deride his sacred rites ?
I, too, despise the Roman gods, and laugh
To see an homage where contempt is due.
And if within their sculptured fanes I bend,

Oblations pour, or incense burn—what then ?
'Tis but a custom, and I fear offence.

SYLV. And if some day——

PUB. I must dissemble, and
In silence wait for better times. I am
The only son of Rome's proud prefect, who,
With cruel zeal, defends the ancient rites.
His wrath—a son can do no less—I fear.

SYLV. In faith, which rests confidingly on God,
Thou wouldst find strength. Her stronger arm can lift
The heaviest burden that oppresses man.
I, too, and this poor child, alas ! must bear
The awful anger of a father. Yet,
With Heaven's grace, we trust to conquer, though
The cords of nature sunder in the strain.

FAUST. O happy victory ! when all our heart
Has treasured up of love, is humbly poured
In full libation to the Lord of all.

PUB. (*Aside.*) [O generous youth ! my weakness
grows ashamed.]

Forbear, my friends, forbear to press me more,
Whom fate has bound with her unyielding chain.
Thy God forgive me if, to-day, His voice
I can not, will not hear : or let Him give
That stubborn virtue which resides in you !

    SYLV. Beware !   He speaks, who will not be refused.
       He, when *thou* callest, may refuse to hear—
       To late repentance turn a deafened ear.
                      [*Enter* ASTERIUS.]

SCENE III.

SYLVANUS, FAUSTINUS, PUBLIUS, ASTERIUS.

    AST. Make haste, young masters, to return ; or else
Your father——

    SYLV. (*In painful surprise.*) Father ?

    FAUST.   He has come at last !
Oh, quick—I long to see that lovèd face.

    AST. His eagerness outran his messengers.
First, in Bellona's temple, grateful rites
He pays for safe return, and then he hastes

To fold you in a father's warm embrace.
I go at once, nor should you tarry long.   [*Exit.*]

SCENE IV

SYLVANUS, FAUSTINUS, PUBLIUS.

PUB. Sylvanus, friend, why pensive thus, and sad,
Whose joyful feet, like winged Mercury's,
Should fly to greet thy parent home ?

SYLV.   Nor thou
Dost know, still less couldst understand, what thoughts,
In strife perplexing, trouble my poor soul.
How deep the love I bear that father, oh !
Great Heaven knows !   What rapture mine, to rest
My head upon that bosom, seamed with wounds !
But, ah ! the wound that we, his sons, must give,
Deep in his soul must leave its rankling smart.
This holds me pensive now, and sad.

PUB.   And why
Inflict the wound ?   Within thy bosom locked,
The secret of thy faith can do no harm.
Exterior semblance can not injure thought.

Sylv. How little knowest thou of Christian faith,
Which, like the lily, fair without, is gold
Within !   Not hearts alone, but lips, must yield
Respective homage to their Lord.   Alike
Created by the self-same God, they owe
Allegiance—one, undivided, true.
To counterfeit, we hold base cowardice.

Faust. Not only coward he, but liar, too,
Who, but in semblance, should deny his God.
Than which a thousand deaths were better far.

Sylv. God help us, brother, we must go where love
Shall fight with love, and faith with piety.
Farewell, my friend ; remember, that one proof,
Alone, I ask of thee—to hail thee one
In faith, as in affection we have been.
   Farewell, where'er thy charred remains are laid,
My mother—let thy spirit hover round,
Whilst life's swift current bears us on its tide !
   Soon dawn the day that sees my body lying here,
   While, soul with soul, we share a joy that knows not fear
                    [*Exeunt* Sylvanus *and* Faustinus.]

SCENE V.

Publius.

Pub. What courage, and what strength, are theirs !
    No fear
Hath death for them ; no tempting charms hath life.
Some hidden and mysterious virtue dwells
Within the bosom of these Nazarenes.
O blessed youths, who know no doubts, no fears !
And I—must stifle that imperious voice,
Which, low but clear, and never-ceasing, calls
Me to the fuller knowledge of that God
Whom I do fear to know, and fear to flee.
Too well I see what better part were mine,
Were but my courage equal to desire.
    In vain my struggles, vain the sigh for peace ;
Still speaks that voice, whose accents wake remorse.
    O God, if thou art very God, and one,
Be not a tyrant to thy feeble slave !
    Oh, hear my prayer, and grant me peace at length,
    Forgive my error, or impart a Christian strength !

SCENE VI.—*House of Severus.*

SEVERUS.

SEV. At last, my fondest wish is crowned. Once more,
Imperial Rome I see ; and this, my own,
My long-loved home, receives me yet again.
My ears are filled with friendly greetings, and
New honors drop, unsought, from Cæsar's hand.
And yet (*seats himself*) I grieve, my wandering looks
         would seek,
But seek in vain, my buried happiness——
O gods ! ungrateful, unrelenting, harsh !
Wherefore that cruel blow ?——No light is here,
No joy can dwell within these walls, since she,
Who was their beauteous sun, is gone.

                [*Enter* ASTERIUS.]

SCENE VII.

SEVERUS, ASTERIUS.

SEV. Come in, Asterius. Where are my sons ?

AST. I went to warn them of thy quick return.
They come.

SEV. Beloved sons! Sole comfort left
Unto my bleeding heart! Thou canst not know
How little, yet, I brook my widowed fate.

AST. Thy loss, indeed, was great.

SEV.   Lamented spouse!
Three years have fled, and still I feel the pangs
As when, in distant Libya, the news
Shot to my heart, like shaft from Scythian bow.

AST. 'Tis just; and yet, if like myself thou hadst——

SEV. And wast thou present, then, Asterius?

AST. And couldst thou doubt? Thy freedman, and
          yet more
A Christian, I——

SEV.   I knew thee Christian,
And trusted thee, despite the hated name.

AST. E'en to the forum did I follow her,
And, after sentence, stood beside the fire,
From which her gentle spirit fled to Heaven.

Sev. (*Starting up.*) Oh ! horror !   What !   That
  lovely woman form
Enwrapt in flames !   Ah ! grateful Cæsar, this—
Is this thy servant's pay !   Had I but stood
Beside thee then !   But what could I have done
To save my innocent—my Flavia !
'Twas well that distance spared me, on that day,
Thy flowing tears, thy agonizing shrieks.

Ast. I saw no tears, I heard no shrieks ; for she,
With smiles, did listen to her sentence, and
She passed to death with gentle tread, but firm-
Her visage tremulous with joy.   The flames
Sprang up like writhing serpents : shrunk the crowd,
In pity, as in fear : but through that veil
Of quivering flame, I traced her joyous smile——

Sev. No more, Asterius ; oh, spare me that !
The final throes of such a death—and *hers !*
 Yet, tell me.   Did she speak of me ?   One word,
In that her dying hour—though but my name—

Ast. I had not told thee all.   Dost know this gem ?
       [*Giving a ring.*]

SEV. How well I know it! 'Twas our wedding-ring.
When first it sparkled on my Flavia's hand,
How little thought I it would thus return!
Oh, silent witness of our happier hours,
Of all our hopes, of all her faith and love—
                           [*Kissing the ring.*]
And death, alone, shall pluck thee from my hand.
                               [*Putting it on.*]

AST. When last she spoke to me, she drew this ring,
And—"Take, Asterius, take my wedding-ring,
And tell my dear Severus, by our love,
And by our plighted faith——"   [*Hesitating.*]

SEV.   Go on!

AST.   ——" to grant
The dying wish of her, who was his spouse:
Renounce false gods, embrace the faith of Christ."

SEV. (*Agitated.*) Ye gods! her dying wish! when
           naught but truth
Should flow from human lips! Faithful in life,
Would she in death betray? Oh, no! The thought,
Sweet Flavia, forgive! Illusions charmed

Thy fond, poetic soul; bewitched thy mind.
And yet, could she, could any one proceed
With happy eagerness to such a death,
For a mere thought, a fiction of the brain?
No doubt some God—if so, no Roman God—
A sole, all-powerful and jealous God—
Is present in these persecuted crowds,
Who throng to execution as a feast.
I, too, must know Him—knowing, must obey.
My Flavia points the way.　But Cæsar—and
My boys—what would they say, if I should close
The road for them to wealth and civic fame:
If I, their father, leave, sole heritage,
A name of infamy.　It shall not be.
This were but madness, and base treachery.
Fear not, my sons!　Begone, ye crazy dreams!
　　　　Asterius, go seek my boys; I long——
　　　　　　　　[*Enter* SYLVANUS *and* FAUSTINUS.]

SCENE VIII.

SEVERUS, SYLVANUS, FAUSTINUS, ASTERIUS.

SYLV. O father, here! embrace thy sons!

FAUST.　　　　　　　　　　　　Father.

Dear father, wouldst thou know thy son ?   I am
Thy own Faustinus.

SEV. (*Embracing them.*) Oh, my children !   More
Than life I love you.   Come—once more.   My heart
Were empty but for you—this gives me life.

SYLV. No more shall we be separate.

SEV.   At last
My grief may end—in you she lives again.

SYLV. 'Twill be our care, as 't is our fondest hope,
To fill her place, and smooth thy path in life,
That peace and joy may dwell again with thee.

FAUST. Receive, dear father, our most tender love.
                              Kissing his father's hand.]

SEV. (*Holding him by the shoulders.*) Faustinus—
                    dearest child !   Thy mother's look
Is in thine eyes, her smile upon thy lips.
Time seems to mould thee to thy mother's form—
Her very self in miniature.

FAUST.   Oh, may
Kind Heaven grant my heart may be like hers ;
Then would the bud be worthy of its stem.

    SYLV. (*Aside.*) [Dear mother, from thy seat of bliss,
          look down,
And let thy glance illume his darkened soul.]

    SEV. If fate adverse still dog my wearied steps ;
        If storms assail, and darkness cloud my life,
        At least, may you escape the fatal strife.

ACT II.

———◆———

SCENE I.—*House of Severus.*

SEVERUS.

SEV. Returned from distant climes and troubled cares,
I thought, in vain, a truce was made with grief.
A cruel fear, a dread suspicion reigns
Within my bosom, boding future woe.
Can it be true?   Are they, too, Nazarenes—
And traitors to their country, and to me !
Their silence, broken words, embarrassed looks,
Breed quick suspicion of that odious faith.
To fill my cup, this bitter drop was poured.
And still it may not be—my heart is sore,
And from a shadow fears a coming blow—
And yet the doubt alone is torturing—
I'll put them to the proof, and know the worst.

                              [*Enter* VALENTIUS.]

SCENE II.

SEVERUS, VALENTIUS.

VAL. Me, Rome's Prefect, and Severus' friend,
Imperial Cæsar, greeting, sends to thee.
Thy grateful service he has marked, and culls
A brighter laurel to adorn thy brow.
He hails thee Questor, and awaits thy troth.

SEV. For this new honor, undeserved and high,
Severus thanks his Emperor; the boon
Accepts, and swears eternal fealty.

VAL. All Rome applauds thy worth, thy valiant deeds:
Permit thy friend to join them, and to wish
With growth in years, still greater growth in fame.

SEV. Yet, may not these be Fortune's treacherous wiles,
Who smiles on him o'er whom she lifts her sword?
Ah! from that day that darkened life to me,
I fear no ill, and honors I contemn.

VAL. Drive far from thee that harpy, bird of gloom,

On Pluto's shores to find its lawful prey.
The past be buried, live unto the day,
And dull in public life thy keener grief.

SEV. Sole comfort of my heart[1] as Flavia,
Now snatched from me by cruel hands.

VAL.   And why
To Cæsar's edict would she not conform !
And why refuse to bend her stubborn knee—
To offer incense to Olympian Jove ?
I saw how Rufus, Prefect then of Rome,
By friendly counsels, and by logic arts,
Appeals, that move the Mother and the Spouse,
Essayed to shake her purpose, and to save——

SEV. And why, Valentius, do such victims bleed ?
Can gods approve this sacrifice of blood !
Throughout the empire, see the ensanguined stream ;
It blots the country with a loathsome stain.
  In Libya, I saw them led in crowds
To death, and yet that cruelty was vain.
For one that died, a thousand sprang to life,
And owned the God of those, who smiled at death.

Methinks from out their ashes, and their blood,
The others take new hope, and life, and strength.

VAL. The throne is not secure, the country safe,
Until that sect rebellious is no more.

SEV. Oh, flimsy veil for cruelty!   And when
Was civic peace disturbed by Nazarene?
In battle lions, and in peace as lambs,
What law convicts them, or what crime is theirs,
Who unto Cæsar render Cæsar's due?
    I love them not—and little cause have I—
My country's gods I serve, but still,
I shame to see the wrongs they have to bear.

VAL. Not ours the fault!   Executors are we
Of him, who sways the sceptre of command.
Small need has he of argument, I trow,
To whom Maxentius is Lord.   'Twere best
To spare his words, and make his actions speak.
    Leave we this mournful topic.   Thou must go
Take auguries for thy new dignity,
And offer sacrifice on Palatine
Unto the genius of the Emperor.

SEV. 'Tis due ; the sacred rite must be fulfilled.
Let some one call Sylvanus here ! My sons
Shall bear me company. (*Starts, and then, aside.*) [The
       die is cast.
And now, too soon, my doubt shall be resolved.
Oh, how my bosom throbs with anxious fear !]

SCENE III.

SEVERUS, VALENTIUS, SYLVANUS.

SYL. What is thy wish, my father ?

SEV.   Cæsar sends
Me greeting, and confers the Questorship.
As is the custom, I renew my oath,
And sacrifice to his divinity.
Thou must with me beside the altar stand ;
Thy loving hand shall my libation pour.

SYL. Forgive me, father, but it can not be.

SEV. Why not, my son ? I bid thee speak.

Syl. (*Calmly.*)   My God—
The one, true, only God—forbids.
Him I adore, and Him I must obey.

Val. (*Pretending sorrow.*) Great Jove! what do I
        hear!

Sev. (*Aside.*)   ['Twas this I feared.]

Val. (*To* Sylvanus.) At least, keep silence.

Sev. (*In despair.*)   It is useless now——
(*To* Sylvanus.) And so—thou art—a Christian!

Syl.   Father, yes!

Sev. I feared it—and the thought was as a worm
Had crawled into my heart and nestled there.
That thou wouldst boast it thus—I never dreamed.
Ungrateful child! Come, rip my bosom up;
Tear out thy father's heart; thy God accepts
Such grateful offerings—who bids a son
Turn traitor to his parent—graceless child!

Syl. Oh, father, would that thou couldst see my heart,

And know the anguish which thy words inflict.
Enough it were that I should see thy pain :
This keen reproach, this name of traitor—no!
Ah! tax me to the uttermost.   My strength, my life—
In any lawful mode, I'll give to thee,
And think the service pleasure—all but this !
To share in impious rites, renounce my faith !
I were unworthy thee, to act this lie.

SEV. Keep silence, shameless one!   Ye cruel gods!
Pursuing still the victim of your wrath !

VAL. Oh, wretched man !   (*Aside.*)   [I have him in
              my hands—
At last !]

SEV. Valentius, pray keep my shame
Concealed.   By all our early friendship, and
By thy own son—may he be ever true—
Expose not this corruption of my blood.

VAL. Fear not, my friend ; repose thy trust in me.
By all the gods, I swear to shield thy son.
                    [*Takes* SEVERUS' *hand.*]
I would not leave thee, but that I must go

Where duty calls me, to the Palatine.
And think not all is lost. A father's words
Are powerful, and he will yet obey. [*Exit.*]

SCENE IV.

SYLVANUS, SEVERUS.

SYLV. (*Aside.*) [O Lord! be present now, to keep me
    firm.
And, mother, let me feel thy prayers!]

SEV. (*After a pause.*) My son,
Whence comes this cruel blow which thou hast aimed
At one, who gave thee life, and loves but thee?
In thee was laid my last, faint hope in life;
My wearied and grief-laden soul reposed
On thee, as on a firm support; and now
It fails—and what have I to live for more!

SYLV. Alas! dear father, spare me thy reproach.
I say it in the sight of God, my heart
Knows nothing dearer on this earth than thee,
Thy happiness, thy will, thy slightest wish.

But yet, I speak it in all reverence,
To break with Him, who made both thee and me ;
Adore false gods, a senseless stock or stone ;
By slightest gesture, to pretend the act—
This, hope it not—for this I must refuse.

SEV. (*Walks up and down.*) This fearful secret should
    have been concealed.
'Tis true, Valentius is my friend, and pledged—
And yet, who trusts a courtier's word?—In youth
We had some angry passages—if now
He sought revenge! [*Stops, looking at* SYLVANUS.]
    Why did I send for thee!
I might have still deferred the proof. And now,
Should he prove traitor, and repeat thy words,
What cruel destiny, my son, were thine!

SYLV. That thought, to one who rests his trust in
    God, '
Should bring no care. Such death were happiness.

SEV. But can thy God demand my ruin, too?
For, know, I should not long survive thy death.
Despair and shame would cut the mortal thread.

Or if my callous heart refuse to break,
I'll find a steel to give my spirit way.

                        [SYLVANUS *appears shocked*.]

SYLV. (*Aside*.) [Support me, Heaven; bid this wind
    be still!
Oh, save me, or I perish!]

SEV.   I read thy soul—
It longs to yield—oh, give thy feelings way!

SYLV. Beloved father, no! What first I said,
That must I say; nor can I change one word.
But should the Christian's triumph, death, be mine,
I pray thee, father, yield not to despair.
There is no shame, where guilt is none. Oh, live—
And live for better days, when I from heaven——

SEV. If, in thy fancied triumph, thou art brave,
And scorn the torments, which must purchase bliss;
At least for me—for thy old father's sake—
Forbear. Give me some hope—the slightest hope:—
My son—Sylvanus, I conjure thee—speak.
Can nothing touch thy heart? Well, then—behold
(*Kneeling*) Thy gray-haired father at thy feet—my son.

SYLV. (*Starting back.*) My father, oh! my father!

SEV.   See—my tears
Have wet the place where thou didst stand.

SYLV.   Ah, rise!

SEV. (*Rising.*) An if thou hadst a tiger's heart,
    'twould yield!

SYLV. Oh, father, mercy!—hear me!——

SEV. ʻ   Grant my prayer!

SYLV. Ah, spare me—'tis in vain—this heart may
    break—.
But e'en for thee, it must not slight its God.
Forsake thy errors for the living truth :
Renounce those lustful gods, to follow Christ,
And then, ah! then, indeed, thy grief shall cease.

SEV. Ah, cruel one! and dost thou mock my pain?
Insult thy father's woe? (*Sees* FAUST.) Faustinus, come—
My child, come, join thy tender voice with mine.
                    [*Enter* FAUSTINUS.]

SCENE V.

SYLVANUS, SEVERUS, FAUSTINUS.

FAUST. What is the matter, father?

SEV.   This, my son:
Thy brother has renounced the gods, and joined
The impious sect of Nazarenes.   His crime
He boasts, in spite of all my prayers and tears.
Join thee with me, to touch this heart of stone.

FAUST. The self-same faith is mine.   Its sacred seal
Within my heart, as on my brow, I wear.
                    [*Signing the cross on his forehead.*]

SEV. Thou art a Christian!   Thou!

FAUST.   Dear father, yes.
It was the heritage our mother left,
In dying, to her sons.

SEV.   Oh, wicked sons!

Oh, traitors both! conspiring to one end!
(*To* FAUSTINUS.) And yet, poor child, the fault was not
    thy own.
Thy innocence, ensnared, knew not the wrong.
(*To* SYLVANUS.) Thou art the guilty one, who led him off.

FAUST. Not so, my father, he was not the cause.
The wrong was all my own, if wrong it be,
To hearken, and to follow Heaven's voice.

SYLV. But from my lips God's sacred word was heard.
(*To* SEVERUS.) On me alone be visited thy wrath.

SEV. Begone! I care not who was wrong. On both
Alike, descend a father's curse. My heart,
That bled with grief, you trample under foot.
Monsters of cruelty! Small mercy can
A pagan father hope from Christian sons!
Insulted gods, assume the quarrel, and
Revenge, alike, your injury and mine!   [*Exit.*]

SCENE VI.

Sylvanus *and* Faustinus.

Faust. (*After a pause.*) Alas! Sylvanus, didst thou
      hear his words?
How terrible! What shall we do?

Sylv. (*Caressing* Faustinus.) Be calm,
My dearest brother, and forget the words.
'Twas but his sorrow spoke, and not his heart.
To Heaven raise thy thoughts. A Father, there,
Condemns the love that separates from Him.

Faust. I see the danger which thou didst foretell.
Our conflict now begins.

Sylv.   It brings a crown!
The struggle will be short, the victory *sure.*

Faust. How know'st thou this?

Sylv.   Last night, as on my couch
I tossed, my sleep was troubled, and my dreams

Were mingled fears of coming ills, and oft,
Methought, I saw my father's angry frown;
When, suddenly, my thoughts took firmer shape.
I stood upon a lovely plain, and all
The earth was smiling, and the sky was bright.
As by some mighty breath, black clouds were blown
Athwart the heavens, and the iightning glared
Incessant, while deep thunders shook the earth,
That trembled 'neath my feet.   I gazed aghast,
Afraid to stay—not knowing where to flee.
Not long the tempest lasted, till, from high,
A mild but steady light appeared.   A cloud
It seemed, but bright and lovely as the moon.
At once the darkness fled, the lightning ceased,
And all was calm and still.   I looked again :
The cloud was opening, and, within, I saw—
Faustinus, hadst thou seen that vision then !

FAUST. What didst thou see?   Pray tell me, quick !

SYLV.   I saw,
Clad in white robes, with flowery chaplet crowned,
All beautiful and bright, and like a star
Within the cloud—I saw our *mother !*   Yes !

[FAUSTINUS *starts.*]

I saw her as I see thee now.   And she,
Extending both her hands, in each a crown,
Did welcome me with smiles to paradise.
And I, all confident and joyful then—
" Oh, pray for father and obtain his grace."
She smiled assent, and then the vision fled.

FAUST. How beautiful !   But who are we, O Lord,
That thou shouldst think of us—with honors crown ?
Ah ! would that father understood our hope !

SYLV. We must increase our prayers.   For with our
        God,
Those prayers are powerful which children raise
For parents' welfare, in the name of Christ.

SCENE VII.

SYLVANUS, FAUSTINUS, ASTERIUS.

AST. (*Entering quickly.*) Have you not heard the
    news ?

FAUST.   Has anything——

SYLV. Pray speak, Asterius. What news?

AST.   The house
Is guarded. Soldiers throng the court. I fear,
Young masters, that we are betrayed. Alas!

SYLV. And that they mean to take us hence? What
        then?
Art thou a Christian, and afraid of this?

AST. Your father hurried to the Palatine,
To seek the clemency of Cæsar. But
I doubt if he can gain an audience.

SYLV. And then in vain. Maxentius does thirst
For Christian blood, and deems a traitor and
An enemy, each follower of Christ.

AST. Unhappy father! who will comfort thee!

FAUST. This is the tempest which thy dream fore-
        told.

SYLV. And we are ready, brother, are we not?

4

Come, let us go to meet them.   Let our faith
And hope be seen, too strong for earthly fear.

   FAUST.   They think to kill, but they can not destroy ;
         A moment's torture wins eternal joy.

ACT III.

———◆———

SCENE I.

*Tribunal of the Prefect.   On one side, a statue of Jupiter,
with an altar.*

VALENTIUS, DEMETRIUS, SYLVANUS, FAUSTINUS.

VAL. Confirmed and obstinate, thy sacrilege
Thou wilt not, then, retract?

SYLV.   Nay, call me firm,
For obstinate is he who clings to wrong.

VAL. Dost thou reject the Emperor's command,
And the supreme authority of Jove?

SYLV. And should I fear a senseless block of stone,
Or gold, or silver, work of mortal hands?

That Jove, so terrible, whose awful nod
Should make me bow, was once a wooden trunk,
Cut from some forest tree.   The woodman's axe
Did shape thy god.   He might, had he so willed,
Have hewn therefrom a drinking-trough for beasts.

  DEM. Blasphemer of the gods !   And what, I pray,
Is He whom thou adorest ?

  SYLV.   He ?   The world's
Great architect.   All powerful, He rules
The earth, the sky, the universe.   From Him
We have our life, our being and our strength ;
To Him alone, as to our end supreme,
We must all things return.

  VAL. (*Sneeringly.*) Thy mighty God
Was crucified.   All powerful was He,
And yet a Roman Prefect bade Him die.

  SYLV. He died, because He willed it so.   His love
For men, it was, conducted Him to death.
  He died :—but death was no surprise, and He
Foretold it to His friends, and gave Himself
A willing victim to His enemies.

He died :—and, in compassion for its Lord,
All nature mourned, earth shook, the sun grew dark,
The rocks were riven, and, from out their graves,
The dead arose, and walked with living men.
   'Tis true, He died :—but, as He promised, rose again.
Three suns had not yet set, when from the tomb
Your frighted sentinels beheld His form
In light, and majesty, and splendor rise.
This proof He gave of His divinity,
And can you longer doubt if He be God ?

VAL. But of this God the worship is proscribed.
Its only guerdon is opprobrium.

SYLV. I know, Valentius : our heritage
It is, from one who chose a mortal form,
And lived the humblest of the sons of men.
" The world hates me, and persecutes," He said,
" You, too, its hate and enmity expect."
   This war, envenomed and persistent, proves
The very truth it ventures to condemn—
Our law divine, its author God, as man !
With rack and sword have you destroyed its life,
Its strength but weakened, or its sons dismayed ?

Like mettled steed that breasts the steepy hill,
It finds new vigor in the bloody goad.

DEM. Yet shall it fall: and soon, imperial zeal,
And Heaven's vengeance sear its hydra-heads.

SYLV. Vain thought! for on a rock, immovable,
Christ founded it.   Kings, emperors may rage,
With all the spirits of the deep abyss—
Against His word, Hell's gates shall not prevail.

VAL. Beneath the blows Maxentius has dealt,
Thy vaunted faith is tottering to its fall.
He whom ye call Chief Pontiff of the sect,
Marcellus, spent with hardship, and with grief,
Within Lucina's mansion, breathes his last.
The head laid low, the body soon must die.

SYLV. One Pontiff dead, another takes his place,
Nor fears the death of those who went before.
Their lot, from Peter to Marcellus, shows
A life of labor, and a bloody palm.
The Pontiff changes, but the sacred fold,
In life, and love, and faith, is still unchanged.

He lives, and watches with a tender love,
Who guards the flock He purchased with His blood.
Almighty and eternal God—He smiles
At Cæsar's power, and at Cæsar's pride.

VAL. Base traitor, silence! Thou art here to plead,
And not to waste our time with foolish words.
Then make thy choice : or sacrifice, or die !

SYLV. My choice is made. *I am a Christian.*

VAL. (*To* FAUSTINUS.) More wise than he, seek not
        to share his fate.
Thy innocence and youth forbid his pride.
Submission more becomes thy tender years.

FAUST. Lose not thy time in counsels such as these.
Full well I know that in thy honeyed words,
A more than serpent's venom is concealed.
Be this enough, Valentius, for thee :
In heart, in faith, in purpose, we are one.

VAL. And wilt thou, in the flower of thy youth,
Forego the sweets of life, so dear to man—
The joys, unknown, untasted yet by thee ?

FAUST. A brighter life, with joys a thousand-fold,
Is promised me by Him, for whom I die.
I do not *die*—I only seek my home,
Where grief is not, and bliss forever reigns.
I go to God, and God is paradise.

VAL. What childish dream is this! Back from the
          tomb,
Did ever soul return to give account?
Who told thee this?

FAUST.   'Twas God that told me this.

DEM. The God who liveth in thy childish brain.

VAL. Has death no fears for thee? Thy tender limbs
Are all unfit to stretch upon the rack,
Thou couldst not bear the pain.

FAUST.   I trust in God—
Who made the lion, can at will impart
A lion's courage to the timid lamb.
Nothing I am, and nothing can I do,
But everything in Him, who strengthens me.

VAL. Thou art a very prodigy of strength.
Dost hope thy God will rescue thee to-day?

FAUST. That could He, too, and He has done it oft.
But far from me to ask the miracle,
For death, to Christians, is the door to Heaven.

VAL. Well, let thy fond imagination play
In airy dreams like these. I, too, would seek
Elysium, but wait a safer ford.
Go thou before, and send me messengers,
Or come thyself, and tell me of thy trip.

SYLV. Valentius, thy mockery forbear!
We go to death—our triumph, not our loss.
But thou, Valentius, truculent and fierce,
Relentless persecutor of the faith,
Think not, hope not, His judgment to escape,
To whose all-seeing eye naught is concealed.
Beneath His altar stir the martyred souls,
Whose bodies, here, were all agape with wounds.
Their blood is on thy hands; that blood doth cry
For vengeance unto God. Though long delayed,
It comes at last, for vengeance is the Lord's!
Thou art our judge, and we thy victims *now*.

5

But know and tremble, for the day shall come
When we shall sit in judgment upon *thee.*

VAL. Meanwhile keep silence, and receive the doom
Which, in the name of Cæsar, I decree.
Convicted, both, of treason, self-avowed,
Against the laws, the Emperor, the gods,
Sylvanus, and Faustinus, ye are doomed to die !
Guards, lead them forth, and rivet on their chains.

SYLV. How I have longed to hear that blessed word !
    Too happy heart, thy prayer, at last, is heard !

FAUST. (*To* VALENTIUS.)
    Dispose thy tortures, and thy arts employ,
    For greater torture brings the greater joy.
               [*Exeunt, with guards.*]

SCENE II.

VALENTIUS, DEMETRIUS.

DEM. Thou wast too lenient with their insolence.

VAL. The foolish rhapsody of braggart youth !

At other mark my shaft is aimed : to reach
A father's heart by striking at his sons.
Of old, he merited my hate ; and I
Concealed the anger, which I could not wreak,
With gentle arts, and polished words, until
He did esteem me for his dearest friend ;
But in my bosom still I fed the flame.

Dem. And what is thy intent ?

Val.   To ruin both
The father and his sons ; suspicion's seed
To sow in Cæsar's breast—a fertile soil.
His children's crime at once suggests a charge ;
And when despair and frenzy ply the scourge,
I doubt not that his confidence in me
Shall utter language——

Dem.   Hush ! thy Publius comes.

Val. We must dissemble.

SCENE III.

VALENTIUS, DEMETRIUS, PUBLIUS.

PUB.   Father, I have come
To supplicate thy mercy for my friend.   [*Kneels.*]

VAL. Arise !

PUB. Thou knowest how he served me once,
And how he risked his life to rescue mine.
Since then my gratitude pursued him, and
Attached my heart to his in friendship's bond;
And now for my sake, father, save his life :
Forgive his fault, remit the penalty.

VAL. My son, I need not my affection prove;
Thy least desire would I fain satisfy.
But on this seat of justice, Publius,
The Father is forgotten in the Judge.

PUB.   The judge I seek;
For he disposeth, here, of life and death.

VAL. The laws dispose, not I. And when they ask
For blood, to shield the empire or the gods,
The Emperor's safety, or the country's rights,
I have no choice, and the award is death.

DEM. And now the insulted honor of the gods
Demands that blood.

PUB. And can not that suffice
Which bathes the altar, and the temple stains?
Thy zeal scarce hides thy priestly cruelty.

VAL. Respect, my son, the priestly character!
Thy friendly supplication is in vain.
Sylvanus can not be absolved—he dies.

PUB. And if, repentant, he should make amends,
Condemn his error, and should sacrifice?

VAL. To his repentance mercy would be shown,
And Cæsar's clemency forget the past.

PUB. Permit me, then, to visit him, at least,
And do my utmost to effect the change.

VAL. 'Tis granted. Lictor, see it done.

PUB.   My hope
Is strong and confident ; and friendship's flame
Shall soften him ; and if his will should bend
Faustinus turns with him, and both are safe.

VAL. The gods, propitious, smile upon thy zeal !

PUB. Ye gentler spirits, who on earth protect
The cares and duties of a friendly love,
Assist the effort which affection makes
To sway a heart, which nothing else can move.
Attemper haughtiness, and soften pride,
That he, who careless seems of selfish ill,
And, reckless, casts his life away, may not
Refuse the pleading of his wretched friend.   [*Exit.*]

SCENE IV.

VALENTIUS *and* DEMETRIUS.

VAL. What fools this silly friendship makes of men !
That genial frenzy I have never known,
Which finds its torment in another's woe.

He only is my friend, who is of use
To my necessity. Whilst that exists,
I love : when that is gone, my friendship dies.
This puling son——

DEM.　　　　　And what if he prevail?

VAL. Fear not, my prey shall not escape.　The pride
Of Christians is as hard as adamant.

DEM. Yet I have seen them, at the feet of Jove,
Give up that constancy which was their boast,
And which had seemed invincible to pain.

VAL. Well, be it so!　Yet shall I not despair,
By thousand arts, and thousand ways, to work
The ruin of my hated enemy.

DEM. New stratagems and new assaults may force
Success, and perseverance win its way.

VAL. There is no means which I shall not employ
To bring this hated rival to his knees.

SCENE V

VALENTIUS, DEMETRIUS, SEVERUS, ASTERIUS.

[ASTERIUS *remains somewhat in the rear.*]

SEV. Dost thou contemn alike, Valentius,
The rights of friendship, and thy solemn oath?

VAL. (*Aside.*) [Confusion! he arrives too soon!   Go
   thou!]   [*To* DEMETRIUS, *who withdraws.*]

SEV. Thy oath was given, though it was not asked,
To guard this secret, and to keep him safe :
Thy friendship pledged, by that now perjured hand,
Which thou, in parting, didst extend to me.

VAL. Hear me a moment, and restrain thyself
Whilst I explain.

SEV. Give back—give back my sons !
At least Faustinus—cruel one—release   ·
That child—wouldst tear him from his father's side !—
So innocent, he knows not what he does !

VAL. Be calm a moment, pray!   Thou art misled,
Thou blamest me as if it were my fault.
Maxentius himself hath willed it so.

SEV. The common trick of lawless ministers,
To screen their wrong, invoking Cæsar's name!

VAL. I take no insult from a breaking heart.

SEV. Speak! was it not thyself betrayed my sons?

VAL. Myself!   Why, Rumor, with her thousand
          tongues,
Proclaimed Sylvanus for a Christian.
How many times was he observed to cross
The noted threshold of Lucina's door!
Reveal it—I!   I had too long connived!

SEV. What soft compassion!

VAL.   And Faustinus did
Compel the guards to take him prisoner.
He heaped the foulest insults on the gods;
He would not leave Sylvanus' side, although
The officer, in pity of the boy,

Implored his silence, and essayed in vain
To loose his clinging arms.   What could I do?
The edict is all stringent and precise,
That every one who bears that odious name
Should be, at once, for judgment here arraigned.
Thou little knowest what this trial costs,
How great the pity which I bear for thee!

SEV. Thou hypocrite! think not I am deceived.
Far worse than thy base treachery, is this
Insulting pity.   Do thy worst!

VAL.   Well, then,
The mask that I have worn I cast aside.
Thy enemy I am, and ever was.
Severus, I do hate thee.   If so long,
In vain, I hoped to reach the curule chair,
Aspired to dignities, thou art the one
Who cheated me of my deserts, and gained,
By trickery, the people's suffrages.
Now reap the harvest, where thy seed was sown.

SEV. And couldst thou for so long this venom hide
Beneath a mild aspect and smiling face?
I care not to defend my course, for that

Thy hate permits not, and my grief forbids.
But grant me less than just : on me should fall
The stroke of vengeance, not upon my sons.

 Behold me at thy feet, Valentius— [*Kneels.*]
Discharge upon thy victim all thy hate—
I shall not e'en complain ; or ask my life,
And I will give it thee ; my children spare,
For they at least are innocent, and thou—
Remember it, Valentius—and thou
Shouldst have compassion, for thou hast a son.

 VAL. At last I see thee weep—and pray! Too
   late ;
Weep on ; thy tears are nectar to my soul.

 SEV. (*Rising.*) Ye gods, and can ye suffer this? How
   long ·
Shall this impiety go unavenged !
Are all thy lightnings spent, O Jupiter !
May Heaven make thee wretched, too—and may
That vengeance turn with just recoil on thee
Which thou wouldst wreak ! But no, Valentius,
I rave.

 VAL. Rave on ; thou hast my leave.

SEV.   Forgive
The madness of a father.   Or, at least,
Permit me once again—'tis all I ask—
To see my children.

VAL.   Well, so much I can.
And thou shalt see them—when they go to die.

SEV. (*As stunned.*) Ah! this is more than I can bear!
                    [ASTERIUS *approaches.*]

VAL.   And hark!
I knew thy children had foresworn the gods,
And could long since have proved it, but preferred
To wait thy coming, that I might enjoy
The bitter pangs which thou wouldst undergo—
    [SEVERUS *leans on* ASTERIUS, *gazing at* VALENTIUS
                    as if crazed.]
A widowed father, losing both his sons.
And for this sweet excess of vengeance, I
Could give a kingdom ; and I long to see
The moment, when my hate shall gloat upon
Thy children's death, thy tears, thy broken heart!
                    [*Exit, with lictors and guards.*]

SCENE VI.

SEVERUS, ASTERIUS.

AST. (*After a pause.*) Fear not, my lord, he's gone.
Repose on me—
Lean on my arm

SEV.   Asterius, my heart
Is breaking—oh ! but this, my cruel fate—
Is more than I can bear—Asterius !

AST. Be calm, and by thy side——

SEV.   I can not live—
I will not live—no ! death shall end my pain.

AST. (*Shocked.*) This must not be !

SEV.   And what but death remains,
To whom a longer life were worse than death ?
I will not live to weep for evermore !

AST. (*Doubtingly.*) Severus, hear! I know a remedy.

SEV. And what?

AST.   Forgive thy freedman, if he dare
To speak with frankness. Love and pity prompt
My every word.

SEV.   I know thou lovest me—
Didst thou not speak of remedies?

AST.   I did.
This is the time to think of Flavia,
And of thy son Sylvanus.

SEV.   Loved names!
Sylvanus, Flavia! Like sounds of peace,
They seem to lull the tempest raging here.

AST. Thy servant speaks the truth, Severus, which
A long experience has taught. Our God,
In this the instant of thy greatest need,
Alone can comfort and restore. Accept
The gift He offers—faith! Bow down, adore!

SEV. What change is this? The thought alone has brought
A sudden calm. But how—I can not think—
And should I then——

AST. (*Aside.*)   [O God! assist him now,
And save.]

SEV.   What didst thou say, Asterius?

AST. Thou canst find comfort in our blessed faith.
If the soul's grief it does not all remove,
Its bitterness it softens and controls.
It lightens suffering, by showing us
His image, who for us was crucified;
And by that hope, reposing in our breast,
Of an eternity of happiness,
It calms the soul, and satisfies the heart.

SEV. (*Passionately.*) Ah! if thou art a very God, and true,
Whom they, my sons, so fervently adore,
In this, the moment of my deepest grief,
And doubt perplexing, turn a piteous eye:
    In suppliant faith most humbly I implore,
    Resolve the doubt, and peace again restore!

ACT IV.

———◆———

SCENE I.—*Prison.*

SYLVANUS, FAUSTINUS, PUBLIUS.

PUB. Sylvanus and Faustinus! loved friends——
(*Aside.*) [Oh, how my bosom throbs—I tremble, while
They seem so happy in their chains.]

SYLV.   Thank God!
I see thee once again, before I die.

PUB. (*Aside.*) [What tranquil happiness illumes his
            face!]

SYLV. This is the moment of our last farewell—
The last that we shall utter on this earth;
Oh, make it not eternal, I conjure!
But why this silence, and these broken words?

PUB. I do not know.   A more than human light
Is radiant in thy eyes—it dazzles me.
I thought to see thee prostrate on the ground,
And groaning in thy fetters, whilst I see
A happy calm, and such a beaming smile
As never yet I saw upon thy face.

SYLV. And should I not rejoice, who stand upon
The very threshold of eternal bliss?

PUB. And dost thou still persist?   Dost thou intend
To kill me with despair?

SYLV.   Despair!   For me?
What evil canst thou see in death?   Oh, if
One ray of that celestial flame, that burns
Within my bosom, could illumine thee,
Then shouldst thou see how beautiful is death
To him who suffers for the sake of Christ:
How light and fleeting is the mortal pain,
Which ushers us into eternal joy.

PUB. I came to reason and convince.   I thought
Success was certain—but, I know not what
Confuses me—prevents what I would say.
6

SYLV. 'Tis God, who keeps thee silent, that His
        voice
May secretly be heard.   Thee, fugitive,
He follows; He would have thee wholly His.
Then yield thee to His love, embrace the truth,
Which Christ now offers thee; and thou shalt feel
A happiness which earth can not afford.

    Refuse—thou losest Heaven and thy friend;
No hope of meeting, then, forevermore!
Oh, Publius, beneath thy feet is hid
A raging sea of flames, which from their bed
Leap up, and roaring, seek thee for their prey
Above thee, Heaven—an eternal crown!
Which is thy choice—resolve!

    PUB. (*Hesitating and embarrassed.*) Pray, give me
        time—
My mind is troubled, and my heart oppressed—
I know not what to say, or do—

    SYLV.   Thou doubtest still?—
Thou wilt not speak?—and wilt thou, then, refuse!
And must I give thee up!—Well, then, farewell!
My friend no more!—I go alone to Heaven.

PUB. Oh no, Sylvanus, stay—I'll go with thee—
Thou shalt not part with me forever—stay!
And yet, I fear——

SYLV.   What fearest thou?   If, on
A battle field, the gleam of flashing swords
Were in thy eyes, then were it shame to fear.
And now, when great the price of victory,
As God is great, how canst thou be afraid?
           [PUBLIUS *remains, looking up to heaven.*]

SCENE II.

SYLVANUS, FAUSTINUS, PUBLIUS, VALENTIUS.

VAL. Well, art thou satisfied, my son?   'Tis time
That we proceed to judgment else.

PUB. (*Slowly, with great joy, and calm.*) I am.
My efforts have attained complete success.

VAL. (*Aside.*) [Perdition!]

SYLV.   Publius, why, this is false!

Pub. I utter but the truth.   The Lord is good!
One thing I sought, a greater I have found:
That would have been thy *loss*—this is my *gain*.
In darkness groping, I have seen the scales
Drop off, that hid from me the light of truth.
Yes! I am satisfied; I want no more.

Sylv. Can this, indeed, be true!

Val.   What thing is this!
Art thou——

Pub.   What *they* are, such am *I*,
Adoring one, true God, the crucified.

Val. (*To* Sylvanus.) Perfidious wretch!

Sylv.   Oh, joy of joys!   My friend,
My brother!

Pub.   Brother, yes!   Faith makes us so.
One thing alone I envy thee—thy chains.
                         [*Kissing the chains.*]

VAL. What holds me, wretches, that I do not
      plunge——
The furies seize you both!

FAUST.   No doubt the prayer
Was heard, which I was breathing unto God,
That He would give assistance to thy words.

VAL. (*To* FAUSTINUS.) Thou viper, cease! Come,
      Publius, I see
The trick. This is some stratagem to save
Thy friend.

PUB. No, father, but to save myself.
No trick, no stratagem, to God I swear,
Who sees my heart, who can not be deceived.

VAL. Thou, too, wouldst boast!—Ah! woe is me!—
      But stay—
I suffocate with agony and rage—
Thrice-sodden fool, to let him come!
(*To* SYLVANUS.) And thou, the hated author of my
      wrong,
Thou infamous seducer, dost thou laugh—
And mock my sorrow with thy wanton joy!

SYLV. May God preserve me from such heinous sin!
I grieve for thee—for him, I must rejoice.

PUB. I never hoped to feel as now I feel.
I never could have thought the Lord would give
Such joy to those who love and worship Him.

VAL. Silence! Add not insult to injury!
Mock not thy parent's shame! Here, guards, lead forth
This crazy fool, and lock him in his room.

SYLV. Fear not, my friend, for He will strengthen
                        thee
Who willed to save.

VAL. (*To the guards.* Hold! (*Aside.*) [I can but try.]
I wish that in another's fate, he learn
To fear his own. Return to the tribune.
(*To* PUBLIUS.) Come thou with me. (*Going.*) There,
                        let the criminals
Be brought. (*Stops.*) Too little for my vengeance, now,
Were death. Slow torments shall prolong your lives;
        And scourge, and rack, and torture shall assuage
        My fury, till each moment seem an age.
                                [*Exit, with lictors.*]

SCENE III.

SYLVANUS, FAUSTINUS.

SYLV. Oh! how my heart exults! My friend is
       safe,
And we at last may die the martyr's death.
Oh, that kind heaven would but send a ray
To chase the darkness from our father's mind.
O Lord! this yet remains, and this alone,
To make the ecstasy of death complete.

FAUST. (*Smiling.*) Oh, thou of little faith! Hast
       thou forgot
How mother smiled to hear thy filial prayer?
Her smiling welcome shows the prayer was heard.

SYLV. 'Tis true; but I could wish, before I die,
To see, with my own eyes, this happy change.

FAUST. Who knows! For He, who holds within His
       hand
The heart of man, can turn it as He wills.

Hard though it be, His slightest touch can make,
From out its rock, the living waters flow.

SYLV. To thee, O God, I bow; thy will be done;
But let my blood ascend unto thy throne,
And there cry pity for my father's soul.
Unworthy though it be, I offer it
In union with thy Son's.

FAUST.   Sylvanus, hear!
The doors are opening—the time has come.

SYLV. Mother, assist us with thy prayers.
      (*To guards.*) Welcome,
My friends. My dear Faustinus, let us go.
The way is very short from earth to heaven—
Though short, 'tis very sweet, if we but recollect
The way He trod, who died on Calvary.
Condemned by Prefect and the vulgar throng,
      He, too, bore insults and a people's scorn:
      A reed His sceptre, and His crown a thorn.
                        [*Exeunt omnes.*]

SCENE IV.—*Tribunal.*

VALENTIUS, PUBLIUS, DEMETRIUS.

VAL. A heavy burden is imposed on me,
Demetrius, to judge my flesh and blood.

DEM. Great Jove! why, what has happened?

VAL.   This—
This wretched boy, Sylvanus has beguiled
To join that loathèd sect of Nazarenes.

DEM. Oh, Publius, can this be true?

PUB.   Beguiled!
I saw the truth which Heaven's light revealed.

VAL. Canst thou not hold that serpent tongue of
          thine,
Whose every accent is a venómed sting?

DEM. And thou, of gentle blood, to whom the gale
    7

Of Cæsar's favor, and thy father's fame,
Blows so propitiously—wilt thou forego
This promise of thy future, and forsake
Thy country's faith, the faith thy fathers held?

VAL. How can I meet Maxentius, when he
Shall hear that I, whom he has held
All worthy of his confidence, have bred,
In my own son, a traitor to the throne?

PUB. A traitor, me!　Oh, father, surely thou
Must know that Christians, who are truly such,
Esteem that duty sacred which they owe
Unto their lawful prince.

VAL.　　　　　　　　Their usual boast!
Their words are honey, and their hearts are gall.

DEM. But, Publius, reflect; thy guilty course
May haply cause the Emperor to doubt
Thy father's honesty.

VAL.　　　　　　　　The thought alone
Has made the blood to boil within my veins.

Thou canst not, and thou shalt not, be a Christian!
'Tis my command.

 PUB.   Which I can not obey.
More holy and more awful is His will,
Who wills me Christian—*Him* I obey.

 VAL. Oh, monster! born for my disgrace and shame!
And for this sect, so obstinate and vile,
Wilt thou forsake thy father! Be it so!
If thou canst trample upon nature's laws,
I, too, can stifle in my heart a father's love,
And rise superior to its slighted voice.
Great Cæsar's favor is a deity,
Upon whose altar I can sacrifice——
Alas! what do I say—— Which is thy choice?

 PUB. My choice is made, and I will follow Christ
Where'er He leads me, though it be to death.

 VAL. Enough! and thou hast conquered, Nazarene!
Thine be the victory—I shall have revenge.
 Lead forth the criminals! Be seated!
        [*To* DEMETRIUS.]

DEM. (*Aside.*)   [Gods !
Have mercy, and assist this wretched man !]

SCENE V.—*Omnes.*

[SEVERUS *and* ASTERIUS *enter from the side opposite to*
    SYLVANUS *and* FAUSTINUS. ASTERIUS *remains in*
    the rear.]

DEM. Valentius, take heed ; Severus comes.

VAL. Keep back that madman !

SYLV.   Father, art thou come
To seek new torture ?

VAL.   Drive him out, I say !

SEV. Fear not, Valentius.   I have not come
To vent my fury here.

VAL.   What seekest thou ?

SEV. When from my mind the mist of error swept,

The angry passions, which it fed, expired :
Thy enmity and treachery I forgive.
I come to gaze once more upon my sons,
A fond embrace, a father's kiss to give.
And Heaven grant it may not be the last!

DEM. (*To* VALENTIUS.) His grief has touched his
    brain.

FAUST.   Oh, father dear!

SYLV. What can he mean?

SEV.   I am not mad : and you,
My children, do not fear : come to my arms——
'Tis more than I deserve—but let me kiss——
                [*Half kneeling, to kiss their chains.*]

SYLV. What wouldst thou do?   We can not suffer
    this.
I scarcely dare to think it true—— Thy words,
That holy light that sparkles in thine eyes——

SEV. Yes! *I*, too, am a Christian—be content,
Sylvanus—dear Faustinus, doubting still?

FAUST. What can I say? My heart is beating so
With sudden joy! Oh, father dear!   [*Weeps.*]

SEV.   My sons,
I gave you life, but you have given me
Immortal life to-day. Your virtues and
Your prayers first touched my soul, and moved;
Your brave example sets it free this day.

PUB. Thrice happy sons, to give your parent life!

FAUST. My heart is full!

SYLV.   O Lord, most bountiful,
We have not earned such mercy at thy hands!

DEM. Valentius, arouse thee!

VAL. (*Aside.*)   [I am stunned;
Rage and grief, confusion and despair,
Commingling in my bosom, wage a war
Implacable and fierce.] (*To* SEVERUS.) Thou crazy
          fool,   •
I'll make thee feel——

SEV.   Thou canst not make me fear,
For, Him alone I dread, who can condemn
The soul and body to eternal flames;
But thou, who canst but torture this poor flesh——

VAL. What insolence! How darest thou speak thus!

SEV. I speak as unto one who fears not God.
And yet not I—God's spirit breathes in me.   .
And you, my sons, my glory and my shame,
Christ's martyrs, deign to pardon and forget
That, in the frenzy of a stricken soul,
I used such foolish words, and threats, and oaths.

SYLV. 'Tis all forgot; we think of nothing now
But seeing thee a worshipper of Christ,
And knowing that we never part again.
Oh, mother! now, indeed, thy prayers are heard!

SEV. And, Flavia, I understand thy gift.
This gem, the symbol of an earthly love,
Which bound us here, thou, dying, didst return
With solemn words, inviting me to come
And pledge with thee eternal vows in Heaven.

VAL. 'Tis time for execution. Part them, guards!

SEV. Why part us now? For, since the crime is one,
The punishment should be the same. Let me,
Though all unworthy of companionship
With them, partake their happy lot.

VAL.   Fear not—
Fear not; it shall be so, I swear. A day
Of blood is this: all pity hence is fled.
The voice of justice shall alone be heard.
  (*To* PUBLICS.) And thou, who for a friend canst thus
          renounce
Thy father—my despair still proves me such—
Go, taste the sweetness of thy friendship now.
Go—with Severus and his sons——

DEM. (*Aside.*)   [Horror!]

VAL. Whom I, to Cæsar and the Gods, and to
My vengeance immolate—go, perjured wretch,
And mix thy impious blood!

PUB.   Oh, blessed word!
Thy error, father, is my only grief.

VAL. Thou still hast thought for me! Too late;
    henceforth
I know thee not—forget thou wert my son.
At least, Maxentius shall see that I,
If from my loyal stem a traitor sprung,
Can use the knife, and lop the accursèd bough.
All else may fail, but loyalty shall stand!

DEM. O soul magnanimous, and fit to share
The fame of Brutus, and of Manlius.
Their worthy deed thou hast this day renewed.

VAL. Let them be led to execution. (*To* DEMETRIUS.)
    So,
My vengeance is complete. And yet I feel
Within my heart the bitterness of death.
      [*Exit, with* DEMETRIUS *and lictors.*]

SYLV. Our race is short, and Heaven is the goal.
    Oh, father, brother, friend, rejoice : the sword
    Shall consecrate us victims to the Lord.

FAUST. Oh, mother, we do come at last. I see
    The golden throne where I shall sit by thee.

Ast. Go, blessed martyrs, and beside the tomb
Where I will lay your forms, I'll pray and wait.
Forget me not, an exile here below.
    The martyr's relic is the altar's prize;
    His death must teach us how to gain the skies.

Sev. And he who, in the future, hears our story, learns
    What grace and joy for parents, filial virtue
    earns!—

Pub. In Christian hearts what sacred friendship
    burns!

A. M. D. G.

www.ingramcontent.com/pod-product-compliance
Lightning Source LLC
Chambersburg PA
CBHW022009050726
47499CB00008BA/2745